THE ABDUCTED MATE
Lilith Leana

Table of Contents

The Abducted Mate (Alien Erotica, #3) 1
Brief Summary 2
Chapter 1 4
Chapter 2 10
Chapter 3 14
Chapter 4 20
Chapter 5 28
Chapter 6 33
Chapter 7 38
Chapter 8 44
Epilogue 49
Authors Note 52
About the author 53
Also by the author 54
Brief summaries of other Alien Erotica titles by Lilith Leana 55

Acknowledgement

A big thank you to my husband for always believing in me and never making me feel like I couldn't do it.

I also want to thank Ada Stuart and Courtney for being awesome Beta readers!

Cover art

Cover art by the talented Misteluna

Cover design

Lilith Leana with Canva

Brief Summary

Haydée is abducted from her bed without her glasses and dropped in the middle of an alien fighting arena. When she thinks her life is over, a gorgeous green, blue catlike alien claims her as his prize. He protects her, and when his crew rescues them, she wants to stay with him but also wants to go back home to her family in Paris.

Ira immediately recognizes the human woman as his long-awaited Mate. He protects her and wants to keep her safe forever. When their ship flies to Earth to reunite her with her family, he doesn't want to let her go.

Will Haydée follow her heart, and stay with the alien or her head, and go back to the only city she has ever known?

Excerpt:

"Hi," I said, suddenly breathless.

"Hi," Ira said.

"It is good to finally see all of you," I said.

Ira nodded. "It is good to be able to speak to you. I feel like I have so much to say, but every time I look into your eyes, the words leave me."

"Oh, then maybe you should close your eyes to talk to me," I said, feeling a blush rise up.

I could clearly see the look in his eyes, as if he didn't care for soup and only wanted me as his next meal. I remembered how his lips felt on mine, how he tasted, and I wanted to experience all of that again, and again until all I could feel was him.

"But I want to see you," Ira said, stretching out his hand and gently caressing my reddened cheek. "All of you."

"I want that too," I said, but my growling stomach redirected the conversation.

TRIGGER WARNING: ABDUCTION

Reader advisory: This story contains explicit sex scenes between a human, and a green, blue catlike humanoid alien. This is book three of the Travelers series, following after the events of The Stowaway Mate and My Alien Pen Pal. It can be read as a standalone.

The Abducted Mate is an 17k word, erotic, scifi, Human FMC, Alien MMC novella. Explicit sex scenes, standalone, no cheating or cliffhangers, child-free ending.

Chapter 1

I woke up in a big bowl. So either I was going to be eaten, or something worse was planned for me. Not sure why those were the first two options to come to mind, but they seemed right. I couldn't concentrate on anything with all the noise surrounding me. It was so loud that my eyes couldn't focus and I was seeing blurry. Oh wait, no, I just didn't have my glasses on. Where were my glasses? I tentatively touched my head to check for my glasses and searched the bowl surrounding me, but I must have been abducted without my glasses.

Had I been sleeping? I remembered getting in bed, and just before I dosed off, a bright white light filled my room, and then... nothing. Something or someone must have abducted me when I had been in bed. The thin floral night dress I was wearing didn't hide much, and I could almost feel eyes burning on my skin. I pulled my arms around me and tried to make myself smaller. Where the hell was I? What happened to me? What were they planning to do to me?

Too many questions whirled around in my head, and I couldn't focus on any of them with all the sounds around me. It sounded like cheering?

Before I could try to understand what it meant, the bowl I was in tipped over, depositing me on the cold, hard floor. I scrambled up, trying to get back into the bowl, but it flew away. I squinted to try to make something of my surroundings, but all I could see were blobs of different colors dancing around me. When a roar sounded and one of the blobs went down, not moving anymore, I realized they weren't dancing; they were fighting. As I looked around, I could feel millions of eyes on me, watching me and the fighting.

I wasn't food; I was the prize for whatever the hell this was.

One of the blobs ran over to me, appearing bigger as he came closer. I could scarcely make out his coloring, but I knew it and all the others surrounding me weren't human. I crouched down, trying to make myself invisible.

Before it could reach me, another blob took it down. One blob after the other went down until only a handful remained. I found myself drawn to one of the blobs that was smaller and leaner than the others, but matched them in fierceness. It was a mix of blue and green and it looked like it swished from one side to the other with a speed that surprised me.

After what felt like an eternity, but was probably only a few minutes, only one of the blobs remained. I squinted, trying to make out who or what it was. It was the biggest of them all and even without my glasses; I knew it was mean. As it came closer, a shiver washed over me and I closed my eyes, accepting my fate. I just hoped it would be over soon. My final thoughts were for my poor maman, who would be left all alone in Paris without me.

An earth-trembling growl made my eyes pop open, and I saw the blue and green figure rise up and sprinting towards the remaining blob. I closed my eyes again, not wanting to see him go down, but I heard a heavier thud than I expected and I hoped it was the massive blob hitting the ground. When I opened my eyes again, all I could see was a massive green chest as the last man standing crowded my body.

He stood up, raising his arms up and growling something to the crowd around us, eliciting a deafening cheer. He had won, and I was his prize. What would he do to me?

Before I could realize what was happening, he picked me up and walked to the side. On instinct, I wrapped my arms around his neck, feeling safe for the first time since waking up in this strange place. I tried to understand those feelings, but too much was happening. I felt like my brain was in overdrive as the figure that held me walked with purpose. I just somehow felt like I could trust him.

We passed a warm stream of air that made me feel clean without bathing. I was thankful for it, not wanting to think about whatever it was that the green alien was probably covered with. His clean scent surrounded me and grounded me. He smelled like the moment after a rainstorm, and something sweet comforting that I couldn't put my finger on. He walked through a long hallway, passing blobs left and right that made strange noises that I couldn't understand but sounded disgruntled.

He carried me inside some kind of room or cell without windows. The door behind us closed with a resounding click, and suddenly we were alone. I held on tight, not wanting to let go. His arms were around me, and when we stood in the middle of the room, he slowly caressed my back with something soft, gently purring. The sound relaxed me enough that I slowly let my death grip on his neck go. I looked up, seeing his face clearly for the first time, and I was stunned.

I already knew he was an alien because of his coloring, but it was fascinating to see him up close. His skin was a vibrant green, and his hair was blue. As I looked higher, I could see two cute triangular cat-like ears popping up from his head. His eyes were yellow and slit like a cat, but oh so expressive. There seemed to swirl so many emotions in them, and I could see that he didn't mean me any harm.

"Thank you," I said in my mother tongue, French.

I wasn't sure what happened, but I somehow knew he had saved my life. If another blob had gotten to me, I was certain they would have taken me the moment we were in this cell alone. But this alien just held me, caressing me and purring to ease my nerves.

He opened his mouth to respond, and I saw a row of razor-sharp teeth glinting in the dim light, but they didn't scare me in the least. A growling sound came out of his mouth that made a shiver wash over me. I didn't want to identify what that sound did to my body, so I looked away.

"I think I can stand," I whispered, and he slowly let me slide down his muscular frame.

He was naked save for a loincloth covering his private parts, and I could feel every muscle in his body stand tight. When my uncovered feet touched the sticky floor, I was suddenly glad that I didn't have my glasses. I took a small step back, so I could still see his face. We weren't so different in height. I usually towered over other men, but he was slightly taller than me, a welcome change. Behind him, a long, furry, blue tail curled upwards, and I realized that must have been the thing he caressed me with. I focused on his face, trying to ignore my surroundings.

"Can you understand me?" I asked.

He made a strange movement with his head, which could be a nod in his culture. I didn't know a lot of aliens, but I knew there were many cultural differences between species.

"Could you maybe nod for a yes and shake for a no?" I asked as I simulated the movements with my head.

He nodded once, slowly, and I smiled for the first time since waking up. "Okay, so we can communicate. I don't understand you, but you can understand me. So where are we, and how are we getting out?"

He cocked his head to the side, looking like an adorable, confused puppy. "Sorry. I'll stick with yes, and no questions," I said with a laugh.

"Do you know where we are?" Nod.

"Can you get us out of here?" Nod.

Excitement bubbled up inside, knowing we weren't stuck in this awful space, and he had some kind of escape plan.

"Now?" I asked, ready to leave this place behind like a bad dream.

The alien shook his head with an apologetic expression on his face. I rubbed my forehead, wishing I had my glasses. I could feel a headache coming up from squinting and trying to focus my eyes too much. He took a step closer, touching the spot I was rubbing gently with one knuckle, careful of his claws.

I could see the question in his eyes and smiled. "Just a headache. The blobs abducted me without my glasses, so my eyes are trying to make up for it, which my brain doesn't like."

He cocked his head to the side, looking very intently at my eyes. "I can see you when you're this close, but everything beyond two meters becomes blurry for me."

He nodded, as if understanding the inconvenience of wearing glasses and not having them. "I wish I was still in my bed and this was all a bad dream," I said with a sigh. "But there is no use in wallowing in self-misery. You can get us out. How long do we need to stay here? A day, a week, a month?"

He signaled with his hand when I said a week, and I nodded. I could survive a week being locked up with this furry green alien. I had no idea why, but somehow I knew I could trust him. The feeling was too confusing to focus on now, so I focused on what I could control.

"Okay, we can stay here for a moment, right? We just need to find some drinking water or something and then we can—"

Two massive blobs in the hallway making awful screeching noises interrupted my words. On instinct, I stepped closer to the cat alien. Without a word, he positioned himself between me and the blobs, protecting me with his body. His blue tail curled around me, comforting me in ways words wouldn't have been able to.

The cat alien made angry growling sounds as the blobs motioned to me and screeched. I couldn't understand the conversation, so I focused on the alien in front of me. He had blue stripes mixed in with the green that covered his back.

The tail surrounding me was massive, fluffy, and a gorgeous shade of blue. As he growled lower, a shiver washed over my back and his tail tightened around me, pulling me closer to him.

The two blobs left again, but I could feel the tension in his back remain. I put my hands on him, feeling him almost vibrate underneath my touch. As I made soothing noises and caressed his soft fur, he slowly relaxed under my touch. The tension bled out of his body, and a soft purring came from him, relaxing me as well.

"What did they want?" I asked.

He turned around, but his tail kept me tucked close to him. He touched my cheek with one of his claws, a sad look on his face.

"Do they want... me?" I asked.

After a moment of hesitation, he nodded. "But I thought you won me. You defeated the other blobs and ..."

I shook my head as fear washed over me. He growled something low, as his tail tightened around me as if trying to say that he would do everything in his power to protect me.

"I trust you," I said.

I'm not sure why I was so trusting of him, but I was. He could have done unspeakable things to me the moment we arrived in this room, but he had been gentle and caring.

"Is there a way to hold them off long enough for us to leave?" I asked.

I could feel a shiver travel through his body, and I knew he was holding something back.

"Tell me. Anything we can do," I said as I touched his muscular chest with my hands.

I could feel him tremble under my touch, but he took a step back, creating some space between us. Feeling the sting of rejection, I let my hands fall away. He kept his tail on the small of my back in a comforting move. With a sigh, he gestured something with his hand. I squinted, trying to understand what he was trying to show.

"What are you..."

He repeated the motion closer to his crotch area, mimicking jacking off, and I took a step back.

"You want to have sex with me?" I asked.

Not that I opposed the idea, but I would prefer to do it somewhere clean and not surrounded by alien blobs who could come in at any moment. He shook his head, then nodded, and shook his head again. He repeated the hand movement in front of his crotch again and then pointed to me.

"You want to come on me?" I asked slowly, and he nodded. "Why?"

He touched his cute button nose, and realization washed over me. "For scent. So they think you claimed me?" I asked.

He nodded, and a look of relief washed over his face. If it meant staying with him and being protected by him, I didn't mind getting sprayed by his seed. Why was I so comfortable with that? I shoved that question in a neat little box in the back of my head - nothing to worry over now.

"What is your name?" I asked, needing to know his name before he came all over me.

A purring came from his chest, that made a smile wash over my face. He reminded me of my maman's old cat, purring when happy and growling when caged in. With his facial expressions and tail movements, I could understand most of what he was trying to say.

He opened his mouth and made a growling, purring sound mixed together. I tried to mimic it, repeating it again and again until he smiled.

"Ira?" I asked to be sure, and he nodded once.

"I am Haydée," I said as I stuck out my hand. "Nice to meet you, Ira."

He took my hand gently in his, careful of his sharp claws. His thumb circled around the back of my hand in a soothing motion. His touch felt electric, exhilarating. Even though I was far away from home, without my glasses, surrounded by alien blobs, I felt safe, knowing I had Ira.

Chapter 2

"So, how do you want to do this? Should I turn the other way?" Ira shook his head, and I bit my lip.

"Can I watch?" I really should not be asking this green and blue alien If I could watch him jack off, but my mouth decided for me.

His eyes burned bright with passion, and he gave me one curt nod. The look in his eyes made me feel warm and safe, and a tiny bit aroused. After what felt like an eternity, he broke our gaze and looked around the room. I squinted to try to make out what surrounded us, but the blurriness remained as blurry as before.

Ira continued to hold my hand as he looked around the room until he spotted something to his satisfaction. His tail swished and a gentle purr sounded from his chest. He pulled me to the side of the room where some sort of bed stuck out of the wall. Ira helped me get on it so I could face him.

He crowded me with his body and his tail, blocking the view from the door. My eyes darted around him, checking if there weren't any blobs watching us. Ira put one claw underneath my chin, gently lifting my face up to him as if saying that I should only focus on him and forget everything around us.

"Thank you," I whispered, wanting this moment to remain intimate.

If we were in a different place, under different circumstances, I would have loved to take him out for a glass of wine and bring him back to my apartment. I focused on that fantasy to try to banish everything around me. I kept my eyes on Ira, seeing his face clearly as he was standing so close.

"It is just you and me. Nothing else matters. When we get out of this, I really need a glass of wine, or bottle to share with you," I whispered.

He smiled, showing off his sharp teeth again. I wondered how they would feel on my skin, and if he would leave little love bites scattered across my body. A shiver washed over me, and Ira furrowed his brows, stepping closer to me, and rubbing my arms for warmth. The shiver wasn't from the cold, but his touch felt so good I didn't want to tell him that.

Ira acted as if we had all the time in the world and weren't locked up in some alien prison. He checked in with me before his hands left me and traveled to his chest. Slowly, he let his hands slide down over his chest lower, and lower until they reached the piece of fabric covering his cock. My eyes followed the path over his muscular green chest, to the blue strip of hair leading my eyes lower. I let my eyes drop down to his crotch area, seeing he was wearing a dark green loin cloth that covered his fun bits.

Slowly Ira pulled the fabric to the side, giving me every opportunity to stop him, but I didn't want to. I needed to see what was hidden behind that green cloth almost as much as I needed my next breath. Instinctively, I leaned closer so my eyes could focus on his cock. His musky, sweet, tantalizing scent surrounded me and made me feel safe.

When Ira revealed his naked flesh, I gasped as his cock was the biggest thing I'd ever seen before. It had a completely different color from the rest of his body. His cock was a soft peach color that stood off against the vibrant green of his muscular legs. The shape was long and pointy, growing wider at the base, and I could already see a clear drop pearl at the tip. I licked my lips involuntarily, imagining his taste, and his purr grew stronger.

Ira growled something low as if asking for permission. My eyes were zoned in on his cock, but I nodded breathlessly, feeling as if no words were appropriate for this moment. His massive hand surrounded his member, not even covering all of it. All of him was just so big, his hands, his cock. How would any of it ever fit? I tried to banish that thought, but as he started to caress his cock with slow, but sure movements, all kinds of images appeared in my mind. I wanted to grab him, kiss him, touch him, taste him.

His claws retracted as he grabbed his hard cock with both hands. The peach color only appeared at every downward stroke but fascinated me. I couldn't look away even if I wanted to. The purring grew louder as his movements increased in speed. My breathing sped up and so did his, and I could feel arousal rise inside of me.

Everything around us disappeared and all I could see and smell was him. My own desire became more urgent, but this wasn't about my pleasure. I wanted to watch him get lost in his pleasure, and for now, that was enough for me. The movements of his hands mesmerized me as the pop of peach appeared ever so often. I had no idea how much time passed, but I could see his tail swish behind him, and his hips thrust faster as his sounds became more urgent.

His hands clenched as his abs flexed, and with a low growl, he came. I focused on his cock as seed spurted out, covering my thin nightshirt. Ira came so much that he soaked my clothes in his cum. I gasped, and bit my lip to stop moaning, but luckily his growls drowned out my sounds.

After a few more jerky pulls, he exhaled and dropped his hands. We were both covered in his cum, and something primal inside of me loved smelling like him. Everyone here would know he had claimed me and he would protect me.

Curiosity got the better of me and I lifted a finger, dipping it in the cooling seed, and brought it to my mouth. Ira stepped closer, purring even louder. I locked eyes with him as I licked his seed off my finger. His taste exploded in my mouth, and I moaned. His cum tasted surprisingly sweet and fresh, similar to lemon drops.

Ira took another step closer, crowding me with his body. He put a finger underneath my chin, lifting it up higher as he leaned in closer until our lips were almost touching. I could smell his warm breath and opened my mouth slightly to welcome him.

He didn't bridge the distance for what felt like an eternity, as if struggling with himself. Before I could say something or lean closer, the lights turned off with a click.

I pulled back, scrambling around me, not able to see anything. Ira's hands grabbed my shoulders, and he purred, calming me.

"I guess it's time for bed," I whispered.

I couldn't see him, but his hands were gentle and the soft sound of his purring reassured me. I patted the bed-like contraption and scooted to the far end.

"I think it is big enough for us both," I said.

His purring grew louder as he climbed up on the plateau. I had grossly overestimated the amount of space we had. Even completely squished against the wall, our bodies were touching everywhere. Ira had just come, but my body was humming with arousal, and I wasn't sure if I was able to sleep with him so close to me. Before my thoughts could come out of my mouth, his tail surrounded me, acting like a blanket, and the tip of it rested on my head.

His presence calmed me somehow, and even though I was God knows where surrounded by awful blobs that probably wanted to do horrifying things with me, I felt safe, knowing Ira was here with me. The stress of the day took its toll and before I knew it, I was asleep.

Chapter 3

The lights turning back on rudely awakened us, almost blinding me. I had slept surprisingly well, considering the circumstances. Ira growled under his breath, turning towards me and pulling me closer. Somewhere during the night, one of his arms had gone under my head and I was now being squished against his body, feeling something very hard poking my belly. His warmth and comforting scent surrounded me.

I snuggled closer to his warm body, trying to forget the world around me for a moment, and feeling safe in his arms. That feeling, unfortunately, didn't last long as the door of our cell opened with a screeching sound. Ira immediately jumped up from the bed, shielding me from whoever had entered our cell.

Ira growled as his tail surrounded me, and he extended his claws. I probably shouldn't be feeling warm inside because of his protective instincts, but I did. The conversation was short, and I didn't understand a word, but the tension in Ira's shoulder relaxed a bit. The door closed, and he turned towards me.

"What did they want?" I asked, looking at his face.

Ira still had sleep in his eyes and his fur stood every which way, making him look adorably disheveled.

"Do I still smell like you?"

He leaned in closer, putting his nose almost against my breasts, and inhaled. The soft purring started again, and with a toothy smile, Ira nodded.

"Good. So they know you claimed me, and I am yours."

His purring grew louder with my last words, and I suddenly realized what I had said, but I didn't regret it. If there was someone to claim me, why not this gorgeous alien? I was single, and besides my maman, I didn't have anyone that would miss me on Earth.

My stomach grumbled, and I realized I hadn't eaten in probably at least a day. Ira turned around and picked something up from the floor. He came closer, and

I realized it was a big bowl with a gray sludge. It smelled foul, and I could not imagine there being any nutritional value in it, but it seemed to be all we had.

Ira retracted a claw and stuck his finger in it. He scooped some of the gray sludge up and presented it to me.

"This is the food?" I asked, and he nodded. "Okay, I am never complaining about my maman's cooking skills ever again."

My mother was not the greatest cook, occasionally burning stuff or under-seasoning them, but this was a whole other ballpark. I closed my eyes and opened my mouth, trying to get it over with as soon as possible. Ira put his finger in my mouth, and I sucked on it, earning a strangled groan from him. I peeked through my eyelids and I could see him stare in fascination at my mouth. I grabbed his hand with mine, dragging it out, letting my tongue flick over the surface. The taste of the sludge was faint, and I focused on the taste of Ira. He was salty and sweet at the same time. Seeing his reaction to my mouth made it taste even better.

I opened my eyes, dipping my finger in the sludge, and lifting it up for him. He didn't hesitate and sucked it into his mouth. His tongue flicked over the surface of my finger, and I could feel the texture that was so different from my tongue. Tingles spread around my body as I imagined it touching me in other places.

Before I could let those thoughts stray too far, he fed me more of the sludge. As long as I focused on his taste, it wasn't so bad. I just hoped it was fit for humans, but being a price in their sick game, I imagined they wanted to keep me alive.

When I had enough, I thanked Ira for the food. He licked off his fingers, so slowly I could almost feel it in my insides, and put the bowl down on the floor again. I was thankful for not having my glasses, so I could just focus on Ira and not my surroundings. It was easy to look at him and imagine us being anywhere else than here.

"I wondered if you would have noticed me if we met on Earth," I mused.

His eyes burned bright, and he gave me one very decisive nod. I chuckled, as I could feel a cozy warmth spread inside of me. "I'm sure I would have noticed you. There aren't too many aliens where I come from, especially not handsome ones like you."

His lip quirked up in a toothy grin as I realized my words. I rolled my eyes at his obvious, content smile.

"Yes, I find you handsome. I am sure there are plenty of space girls that think the same thing where you are from."

Ira shook his head, taking my hand in his, and giving a gentle lick on the top of my hand as if trying to say that there was only me. I ignored the way that made me feel and averted my eyes to look at our hands. They were in such stark contrast with each other. His were big, green, and had sharp black claws attached to the tips, and mine were pale with chipped nail polish on them.

It was hard to sort out my feelings while there was so much surrounding us we couldn't control. This wasn't a date where we could get to know each other. We were in some kind of prison, with evil blobs that wanted to do Gods knows what with me. What if they decided Ira wasn't worth it anymore, and they killed him to get to me? Or what if they decided my time was up, and Ira had to go back to win another price?

A shiver washed over me, with too many thoughts swirling around in my head. Ira's tail caressed my lower back as he stepped closer, lifting my chin with a finger. I could feel my eyes sting with unshed tears.

"I'm sorry. This is just a lot. My head hurts, and I've never even left the city I grew up in, and..."

I shook my head, not knowing what more to say. This was a shitty situation, and I tried to be strong, but it was hard. With unsure movements, Ira stepped closer and pulled me into a hug. I relaxed against his form as he purred, caressing my back with his tail.

"Thank you," I whispered against his chest, feeling the tension drain from my body.

"They should sell your purring on a CD or something," I murmured. "I don't know how you do it, but you make me feel safe."

His arms tightened around me, and his purring increased.

"Will it be long before you can get us out of here?" I asked, looking up at him.

Ira shook his head, and relief washed over me. I could hold on for a little while longer, and just focus on him and how my feelings were growing. I've never felt like this for someone so fast, and it confused me. It was probably due to the environment and my survival instincts, but I had grown attached to Ira in a way I hadn't expected.

"Thank you for being here with me, and protecting me, and making sure I still have my sanity by the time we get out," I said with a shaky laugh.

Ira purred, caressing my cheek with one finger and my back with his tail. I melted against his body, loving his arms and his scent surrounding me. The day crawled by, and I just talked and talked about anything and everything I could think about.

I explained what I did for a living in Paris, looking at numbers on a computer all day in my tiny apartment, and what I remembered from being abducted. I still couldn't figure out how they took me without me waking up, or why they even picked me in the first place. When I talked about the abduction, Ira's tail tightened around me in a comforting way. I loved talking to him and I was sad he couldn't speak to me. Ira looked at me as if my words were as valuable as his next breath, and I knew I would feel the same way about the things he had to say to me.

Time seemed to slip away, and before I realized it, evening had arrived, bringing with it another serving of tasteless sludge. We ate it in comfortable silence, his taste making it bearable. When the food was gone, I imagined it wouldn't be long before they dimmed the light.

"Do you..." I took a deep breath, gathering my courage. "Do you need to come on me again?" I asked.

Ira looked at me for such a long time I was afraid I might have overstepped, but with a small nod and a toothy grin, he accepted my offer.

"Okay," I said with a smile.

We moved back to the bed as we had the previous day. I was much calmer now, looking forward to seeing him overcome by pleasure. He stood in front of me and pulled off the loincloth, exposing his already-hardening cock. The shape, and color of it fascinated me and made arousal rise.

"Can I touch you?" I asked, stretching out my hand.

Ira growled low, almost pained, making me pull back. He nodded quickly, grabbing my hand and pulling me close to him. His purring increased as he let go of my hand, hovering above his erection.

"Growl when I do something you don't like," I said before grabbing his cock.

Ira groaned as his purring became louder and I could feel it vibrate through his cock. I slowly caressed his long, hard length, marveling over his size and imagining how he would even fit inside of me. I barely touched him before his cock throbbed and he came. His seed spurted out, covering my hand and my breasts. I gasped and moaned softly as I looked at his face contorted in pleasure. His whole body trembled as his cock throbbed in my hand, and I gently coaxed out the last of his seed.

"That was really hot," I whispered, suddenly feeling like my voice was too loud for the intimacy of the moment.

Ira purred, breathing heavily and looking at me with so many emotions in his eyes that I had to look away before feeling overwhelmed. I wiped my hands on my clothes, trying to compose myself before looking up again. He was super close to me, his breath fanning my face, and his eyes burning with desire.

"Hi," I said, looking from his eyes to his lips and back up again.

He leaned in closer, slowly, giving me every chance to pull back if I wanted to. I closed the distance between us, pressing my lips against his. I moaned in the kiss, loving the way his mouth felt so different from mine, but somehow fit perfectly.

The lights went out, but I didn't care. I grabbed his shoulders, pulling him closer to me until his body was flush with mine. His tail curled around me as his hands cupped my ass, pulling me up from the bed in his arms. Arousal rose inside of me, as I could feel his cock trapped between us harden against my pussy.

I opened my lips, letting my tongue out to play. Gently, I licked his mouth, trying to coax out his tongue. He purred low, and I could feel it vibrate through me as he opened his mouth. His tongue met mine, and I moaned as I could feel its fascinating texture. His taste and scent surrounded me, and arousal filled me. I wanted more than just kisses, but I needed time to build up my courage to ask for more.

It felt like we kissed forever, but it was probably only a few minutes until we got disturbed by an alarm blaring and the lights turning back on. We broke apart gasping, and I looked at Ira for more information. He suddenly looked very serious and nodded at me. He pulled me close in his embrace, and I knew it was time for our escape.

The doors opened, and without any hesitation, Ira started running. I closed my eyes, putting my head on his chest, just hoping he knew the way and we would be out of this hellhole soon.

I didn't look up from Ira's chest until we stopped running. His heart was beating a thousand miles a minute and his breathing was coming out in pants, but he didn't loosen his grip on me once. When I dared look up, I saw a beam of light catch us, and suddenly we were being transported into the air. I squeaked and put my head on his chest again, closing my eyes, hoping everything would be alright and we wouldn't plummet to our deaths.

Ira gently purred, making my nerves unwind, and letting me know we were safe. Only when I could feel gravity return did I dare to peek out. Solid metal walls surrounded us, and as I looked down, I could see Ira's feet standing on a metal floor. I had no idea what happened or where we were, but I was glad we were out of that hellhole of a prison.

Chapter 4

I didn't dare let go of him just yet, and it seemed he didn't mind carrying me for a little while longer. Beeps and clicks sounded around us and I could feel the ground underneath us shiver as if we were being pulled towards something.

The shivering stopped, and four loud clanks sounded, and then it was eerily silent. One of the metal walls opened with a whoosh and a purple and red form appeared. More aliens. Ira continued purring, so I trusted his judgment of them.

Both aliens made strange sounds I couldn't understand, and Ira answered with his growled words. We moved from the metal room into a long hallway, going through another door until we arrived in a brightly lit white space resembling a hospital room. Ira tried to deposit me onto a bed, but I didn't want to let him go. I knew he was safe, but I didn't know about the others yet.

"Don't let go of me, please," I whispered, looking into his gorgeous yellow eyes.

A shy smile appeared on his lips, revealing his sharp teeth, but they didn't scare me. He nodded once, sitting on the table with me on his lap.

Another figure entered the room, and Ira grabbed a blanket to cover us. I hadn't realized he was still naked, but we had been interrupted just before things could heat up between us. The new figure appeared more human, but I couldn't be sure without my glasses.

"How is she doing?" a female voice asked in English.

I looked up, squinting to try to make out the figure.

"You're American?" I asked in English, recognizing the accent.

Ira gasped, looking at me with wonder in his eyes. "You speak English?" he said in perfect English.

"I can speak English, but I prefer not to," I said with a laugh, not believing this alien could speak perfect English.

"What language were you speaking?" he asked.

"French."

Ira picked up a data pad and pressed a few buttons until a beep sounded. "Do you understand me now?" he asked in perfect French.

My eyes widened and looked at him. "How did you do that?" I asked.

He tapped his head and said. "Translating chip. It recognizes languages and translates them in my head, but I need to upload the full file to speak it. It never occurred to me you could speak more than one language without one."

"I learned it in school," I said, still not believing he just learned a whole language in mere seconds.

The female figure approached, reaching out to the data pad. I leaned closer to Ira, still not trusting anyone else.

"I've always wanted to speak French," she said as she pressed some buttons on the pad and switched to the same perfect type of French. "I'm Maia. What's your name?" she asked, stretching out her hand.

I didn't take it, but I acknowledged it with a nod. "Haydée."

Now that she was closer, I could make out her face. She was definitely human and American. She had gorgeous blond hair and delicate features. Behind her came a massive red figure with horns that looked like the personification of the devil.

"And this is my Mate, Levix," she said, turning towards the red giant.

Even without my glasses, I could see the love radiate from them. The way they gravitated towards each other, and how she relaxed against his touch, was a beautiful thing to witness. I didn't know what a Mate was, but the way she said it made it sound like it was similar to a husband.

"He can give you a translator. That way, you can understand all of us. It is only a little pinprick, and-"

"No needles," I said, shaking my head. "I don't want anything implanted in me." I turned towards Ira, shivering. "Please don't let them."

Ira pulled me closer to him, his tail surrounding me protectively. "We will not do anything you don't want. You are safe here."

"I'm so sorry, I didn't mean to scare you," Maia said, taking a step back.

"You don't scare me," I said with as much pride as I could muster. "Needles do."

I had an awful experience with a doctor growing up, and I avoided them and needles as much as I could.

"Can we let the machine do a check-up of you?" Ira asked. "No needles, just a scan to see if you are healthy."

"Will you stay with me?" I asked, not caring if I sounded weak.

"Of course."

I laid down on the table, while Ira held my hand and a machine whirled above me, beeping annoyingly. The red alien stood on the other side, looking at a screen with Maia next to him.

"You seem to be in good health," Levix said. "The only thing wrong with you is your eyes, and we can fix that easily."

I sat up, pulling Ira close to me, relaxing when he purred. "There is nothing wrong with my eyes. I just need my glasses. If I wanted them fixed, I would have done so a long time ago. Can't you make some glasses with all of your fancy alien tech?" I said, waving around.

"I am sure we can figure something out," Maia said with a gentle smile. "Let's give you guys some food and some rest. I am sure you had a tiring few days."

That was an understatement if there was ever one, but I bit my tongue, not wanting to lash out at this nice lady who just wanted to help in her own way.

"Food would be great," Ira said to Maia, and turned to me. "Maia is a great cook, and she makes human food all the time."

A hot pang of jealousy shot through me at the affectionate tone. I pushed it down, knowing it was ridiculous seeing Maia and Levix together. Somehow, I felt like Ira was mine, and I didn't want anyone else to have a claim on him.

"Do you have a favorite meal?" she asked. "I might not have all the ingredients, but I am quite resourceful."

"Just some soup and bread would be amazing right now," I said.

"I can make soup," Maia said and almost ran out of the room.

Levix followed her in a more leisurely manner, leaving me and Ira alone.

"They seem..." I couldn't find the right words without accidentally insulting them. Considering they saved us from that horrible prison and seemed to be people Ira cared about, I didn't want to get off on the wrong foot.

"They can be a lot," Ira said with a toothy grin. "But they mean well."

"And you care about them."

"I do. They are the closest thing I have to a family," Ira said.

"I can understand that," I said with a smile, petting his tail.

It was strange how I didn't want to let go of him, even though I knew we were in a safe space. It almost seemed as if I was addicted to his presence. The simple idea of letting him go made my heart ache in a way I've never experienced before. Before I could say anything else, the red alien, Levix, appeared again, holding something in his hands.

"Can you try this on?" he asked.

I looked at Ira, and after a reassuring nod from him, I accepted it. It looked like something straight out of a sci-fi movie, but then again, I felt like I was smack in the middle of one. It was a small, metal, circular thing that kinda resembled a crown. I put it on my head, and somehow everything around me suddenly appeared sharp again, as if I was wearing the clearest glasses in the world. I gasped, lifting it up, and making the room blurry again. Putting it back on, I smiled, grateful to Levix, who I could see clearly now.

"Wow, this is amazing," I said. "Thank you."

Levix nodded. "Food is ready when you are."

I looked at Ira, able to take him in fully for the first time. He was gorgeous, and even the sheet covering his equipment didn't deter him from his beauty. I loved everything about him. The green, the blue, all his lean muscles, and his tail. My eyes traveled up to his face, and he caught me checking him out. His grin grew wider and his purring louder.

"Hi," I said, suddenly breathless.

"Hi," he said.

"It is good to finally see all of you," I said.

Ira nodded. "It is good to be able to speak to you. I feel like I have so much to say, but every time I look into your eyes, the words leave me."

"Oh, then maybe you should close your eyes to talk to me," I said, feeling a blush rise up.

I could clearly see the look in his eyes, as if he didn't care for soup and only wanted me as his next meal. I remembered how his lips felt on mine, how he tasted, and I wanted to experience all of that again, and again until all I could feel was him.

"But I want to see you," Ira said, stretching out his hand and gently caressing my reddened cheek. "All of you."

"I want that too," I said, but my growling stomach redirected the conversation.

The slosh we had eaten in the prison seemed to have been just enough to get me through the day. With the promise of fresh soup, my stomach seemed to make itself known.

"I think the soup should be ready," Ira said, offering me his hand to get off the tall bed. "Let's clean up, get some clothes, and eat."

I kinda wanted him to carry me again, but I knew I was perfectly capable of walking. After a quick air shower, that made me feel cleaner than ever, and made my curls bounce again, he offered me a space suit that molded itself to my figure. I was self-conscious of my body, but when I saw the heated look Ira gave me, I didn't mind the curve-hugging suit. He wore a matching one and somehow made the colors of both change to the green color of his skin. Since I was already overstimulated from everything that happened, I didn't even question how it worked.

We went to the dining area, and I was in awe of my surroundings. I was in an actual freaking space ship and I could see everything clearly. If it hadn't started with my abduction, I would have actually enjoyed the experience. Now I was just tired and ready to get home and sleep for a week, preferably with Ira next to me.

The soup was delicious, and the bread was crispy on the outside and soft on the inside. I thanked Maia and her smile was worth it. Ira never strayed far from my side, his tail or hand always touching me, making me feel safe. I wasn't a worthy conversation partner as fatigue took over, and I yawned multiple times in a sentence.

"It is time for us to rest," Ira said to Maia and Levix. "Thank you for the food and the company. Tomorrow, we will meet the rest of the crew."

"Okay," I mumbled, already curled up on his lap, ready to fall asleep.

Ira carried me to his room, purring and lulling me to sleep. He pulled the crown glasses from my head and pressed something on the space suit, that made it more loose like a pajama. I almost didn't feel him putting me down on the bed, but when he didn't join me, I opened one eye. He was standing next to the bed, his hands fidgeting with the space suit.

"Come here," I mumbled, stretching out a hand. "Cuddle with me."

A soft smile grazed his lips as he got on the bed with me after pulling off his clothes. I imagined I would fall asleep in an instant after the events of the past few days, but I couldn't.

"Ira," I whispered, hoping he would still be awake.

"Yes, Haydée," he whispered back, his delicious raspy voice laced with sleep.

"I can't sleep. Could you…" I couldn't believe I was going to ask this. "Could you come on me again?"

I had no explanation for why I asked this, or why I thought it would help me sleep, but as soon as the words left my mouth, something clicked. I could feel his body tremble next to mine, and a soft purr came from deep within him.

"You want me to cover you with my seed so you carry my scent again?" Ira asked.

"Yes," I said, happy the room was dark and he couldn't see the blush creeping up my face.

"I would love that," Ira growled, turning over until our bodies were flush against each other.

His cock was poking my belly and already hardening. I moaned softly as I let my hands travel down over his naked chest to his growing erection. His breathing became more labored, as I could feel the tension in his body. Last time he came almost instantly when I touched him, but I wanted to stretch the experience more this time.

"Tell me if I am doing something you don't like," I whispered as I slid down the bed.

"What… what are you going to do?" Ira asked in a strangled voice.

"I am going to lick your cock," I said, wanting both his scent and taste.

"Oh, by the Goddess. Do humans really do that?" Ira asked in an incredulous tone.

"Yes, and it is quite pleasurable, I have been told."

I grabbed his cock, guiding it to my mouth, loving his scent surrounding me. I didn't know what it was that made me so drawn to him, but his smell was definitely on top of that list. His cock touched my lips and the most guttural sound came from Ira. It throbbed underneath my touch, and I knew that my plan of stretching the experience would be in vain.

"Oh Goddess, your lips are so soft," Ira groaned.

My mouth quirked up in a smile as I opened my lips, licking the tip of his head.

"Was that your tongue? I won't last Haydée. It feels too good with you."

I was done teasing, taking his words for truth, and sucked on the tip of his erection. His taste exploded in my mouth and I moaned around his cock. I could grow addicted to his sweet and tangy taste. His cock was already leaking and more of his taste filled my mouth.

"Haydée," he groaned, sounding pained.

I moaned around his cock, moving my hand and head in sync, caressing and sucking on it. His whole body trembled as his hand reached down, grabbing my head. The purring grew louder and louder until his cock was vibrating in my mouth and I had trouble getting it in deeper.

"It's too good. I'm going to burst," Ira groaned as his hips pushed up, stuffing more of his cock in my mouth.

I wanted to encourage him, tell him it was fine to come into my mouth, and I craved his taste, but I didn't want to release his cock. His body took over as his hand tightened around my head and his hips thrust up. I moaned around his length, sucking harder and caressing him to increase his pleasure. With a guttural groan, Ira exploded in my mouth. I sucked down his cum, but it was too much to swallow. I released his cock, swallowing down what I could as the rest splattered on my breasts.

With a happy sigh, I crawled up, covered in his cum, and his taste fresh in my mouth. Ira grabbed my head and pulled me towards him, crashing his lips onto mine. He didn't seem to mind the taste of his cum as his tongue entered my mouth. I moaned into the kiss, grabbing hold of his shoulders as his tail pulled me closer to him.

His lips left mine, breathing hard. He pressed his forehead to mine. "Let me return the favor, please."

"You don't have to," I said, suddenly feeling shy.

"I want to, Haydée. I need to," he groaned, his body vibrating with his purring.

"Okay," I said with a smile as my body hummed with arousal.

"Guide me."

I opened the space suit with the click of a button and wiggled out of it. I loved the futuristic garment, but I preferred to feel his naked body against mine. Grabbing his hand, I tapped against his nails until he retracted them, and led him down my body in between my legs. Sucking him had made me aroused, and I was already soaked, so close to coming.

"So wet," Ira groaned. "I need a taste. Can I?"

"Oh, yes, please," I moaned.

Ira pulled his hand back up, sucking off his finger, groaning when my taste hit him. His hand dove down again, pushing between my pussy lips, gathering more of my wetness.

"How do I give you pleasure?" Ira asked.

"You are doing pretty good, but circle my clit to make me come," I said as pleasure rose inside of me.

His finger traced my pussy until I jumped up as he touched my clit. His purring increased as he circled the little bud of pleasure.

"This?" Ira asked.

"Yes, Ira," I moaned.

"Is this your pleasure button?" Ira purred.

"Yes, now please, rub it."

"Such a needy little Ma-" he cut himself off before finishing his sentence, but I was too far gone with pleasure to question him.

"Harder, faster," I moaned as pleasure rose inside of me with each swipe of his finger.

I opened my legs, and his tail slid between my thighs, giving me more pressure where I needed it. My hands grabbed his hair, loving the feel of the soft strands underneath my fingers. His body was against mine as his tail and finger gave me pleasure.

I moaned his name as he increased the pressure until I burst. Pleasure washed over me as sounds left me I hadn't made before. Everything with him felt so much better, as if a light had gone on inside of me, recognizing him as mine. My pussy squeezed around nothing as my body trembled with pleasure.

"So beautiful," Ira murmured as the last tremors left my body.

"Can you see me?" I asked.

"Yes," he said, and I could see his teeth glint in the dark. "And you are beautiful when you take your pleasure."

I buried my head in his shoulder, feeling my cheeks heat up. No one had ever called me beautiful as I came.

"Go to sleep," I mumbled.

His laugh vibrated through me, as his arms and tail surrounded me, and in moments, I fell asleep.

Chapter 5

When I woke up Ira was gone, but his side of the bed was still warm. I got up, put my space suit back on, and exited his room. It felt strange not to have his presence close to him. I walked through the hallways as if sensing where to go. I heard voices, and a smile appeared on my face, recognizing Ira's voice, but when I heard my name, I waited around the corner, listening to the conversation.

"Are you sure?" an unknown male voice asked in English.

"Yes, but she doesn't know it yet and I don't want to scare her," Ira said.

"If she is truly your Mate, I understand you need to be with her."

Mate? The word made something flutter inside of me, but I didn't know what it meant. Maia had talked about Levix as her Mate, and they seemed madly in love. Was that what was happening to me?

"Thanks, Zion," Ira said.

The other male sighed. "Everyone is finding a female. Soon I won't have any crew left."

"You know, Levix and Altair will never leave you."

"They might," the male said in a sour tone. "I never thought you would leave me either, but here we are." The silence stretched until the male voice added. "I am happy for you Ira."

"Thank you. You are a good friend, and I am sure you will find your Bond Mate too," Ira said.

The other voice murmured something in reply, and I heard footsteps approach me.

Ira turned the corner, almost bumping into me. His hands grabbed me to keep me steady, and his toothy smile appeared on his face. I did love his smile, and his hands on me, and being close to him made me feel safe even though he was an alien. But what did it mean? Was it just an infatuation and would it pass or was it something deeper?

"Hi," I said. "I woke up, and you were gone."

"I was. I'm sorry. I just needed to talk to the captain about something," switching to French for me.

"What?" I asked.

Ira hesitated, scratching the back of his neck. I didn't want to pressure him into saying something he was not ready for.

I grabbed his hand and smiled. "Sorry for being nosy. Do you want to show me the rest of the ship?"

"Yes. I'll introduce you to Altair and Vivian. Vivian piloted the ship yesterday while Altair flew the escape shuttle."

"I would love to meet them and thank them for getting us out."

We walked through the hallway when my curiosity got the better of me.

"Can I ask why everyone speaks English on the ship? It just seems strange that aliens are talking English when you all have those translator things."

"Oh, that is because Maia wants the kids to learn English as their first language, and we can't give them translators until they are fully grown."

"Kids?" I asked, stopping in my tracks. I couldn't imagine children running around this spaceship.

"Yeah. Maia and Levix have two little ones already and I am pretty sure that during his next heat, there will be a third coming."

The blond woman had seemed like the motherly type, but I just couldn't wrap my head around her compatibility with that giant red devil.

"So aliens and humans are compatible?" I asked.

"Not all, but mated couples are."

So we might be able to have kids? If we were truly mates. My heart fluttered as a whole world of opportunities opened up. I was lost in my thoughts as we rounded another corner and got to the cockpit. A golden, lizard-like alien and a small woman with short black hair were discussing something while looking at a screen, but the giant window overlooking the stars immediately drew my attention. I knew I was in space, but seeing the stars swoosh by was something entirely different.

"Wow, it's beautiful!" I exclaimed, running to the window and pulling Ira with me.

"It is," he said, and I could feel his eyes on me.

I didn't want to look at him, knowing my cheeks were heating up. I focused on the mesmerizing view.

"Even after so many months, I am not used to it either," a female voice next to me said.

I turned towards her, smiling. "I can imagine."

"You must be Haydée. I'm Vivian. Welcome to our cockpit."

"Nice to meet you. Sorry for my lack of manners. I just couldn't look away," I said, my eyes back on the stars.

"Totally understandable. You are welcome to stay here as long as you want," Vivian said.

"Doesn't it make you feel incredibly small to see how vast the world out there is?" I asked.

"It does, but in a good way. It helps reduce my anxiety to know we are not alone and there is so much life around us," Vivian said.

"But not all with the best intention," I said with a shiver.

"You are safe here, and if I know anything about Ira is that he would never let anything happen to his ma..." she coughed, losing the last word.

I looked up and saw Altair pull her towards him. Ira was standing next to me, his tail still tucked around me.

"You will keep me safe, won't you?" I asked.

"With everything that I have," he said, his tone serious and his usual toothy grin absent from his face.

I put my hand on his chest and smiled at him. "I trust you."

"I'm honored," Ira said. "Let's see the rest of the ship and meet the Captain."

Ira thanked Vivian and Altair and showed me the rest of the ship, explaining every room and functionality.

"We used to have a small cruiser with just the four of us, but with Levix finding his Mate, and having children, plus Altair meeting Vivian, we needed more space. Zion bought this beauty last month and now we all have our own wing of the ship."

"He sounds like a good boss," I said.

"He is more than just our boss. He is the captain of this ship and he calls all the shots, but he includes every one of us in his decision-making process. Even though he doesn't like to show it, he truly cares for us as if we were his family."

"So, what kind of jobs do you guys do? Saving damsels in distress from a prison doesn't seem like something fitting this family vibe?" I asked.

"Zion got a tip from an old military contact that humans were being abducted as prizes, so I went undercover to gather evidence to help the law enforcement gather a case. Since we are not aligned with any specific planet or species, we can go where they can't," Ira said.

"So, there were others abducted like me?" I asked, shivering, remembering the panic I felt waking up somewhere unknown.

"Yes, but no one else will get hurt. We handed over all the evidence and they shut down the whole planet," Ira said, as his tail caressed my back in a soothing motion.

"Good," I said, nodding.

We arrived at a big door where Ira pressed a button to make it open up. Behind it was a magnificent study room with a big desk and papers littered everywhere, and a massive window overlooking the stars. The most surprising thing about the room was that there were plants everywhere. I could almost not see the metal walls surrounding us because of all the foliage. Sitting at the desk was a bulky purple alien with four arms and a green buzz cut.

"Zion, this is Haydée," Ira said.

"Nice to meet you," I said.

"You too, Haydée," Zion said as he stood up, motioning with one of his hands. "I would like to formally welcome you to our ship."

"Thank you," I said. "So, when can I go home?"

"To Earth?" Zion asked.

"Yes, Paris. My maman will be worried sick, and I need my glasses and personal things. I appreciate this tech thing, but I really prefer my glasses."

"But you still need to testify," Zion said, crossing all four of his arms.

"Testify? About what? I woke up in a bowl and Ira saved me. I didn't have my glasses, so I didn't even see anything. I could hardly give an accurate description of my surroundings, so what use would my testimony have?"

"I hadn't thought about that," Zion said, rubbing his sharp jaw. "I'll make contact and see what they say. If they agree, we will make the course to Earth. I know Maia has been asking to visit ever since the second little one arrived," he said and a ghost of a smile played on his stern face.

"Thank you," I said.

We went back to the hallway, but Ira was uncharacteristically silent.

"What is it?" I asked.

"Nothing," Ira said, his toothy grin back on his face. "Just thinking about how I've never been on Earth."

"Oh, you'll love it. I can show you around Paris if you want."

"It would be my honor," Ira said.

I smiled back at him, already planning what I would show him of my city and who he should meet. My maman was on top of that list, of course. I know she would be worried if she didn't hear from me after a few days. I worked from home as a freelancer and I didn't have the biggest social circle, so it would be easy to pack up and join him and the rest of the crew on their adventures if they would have me.

Chapter 6

"What part of the ship do you want to see next?" Ira asked after we left the Captain's office.

"I would love to see your bedroom again," I said, with what I hoped was a seductive smile.

I craved his touch again, and knowing we were going back to Earth made me want to make the most of my time on this ship with him.

"We already-" Ira cut off his own words as he saw the look on my face. His toothy grin widened as his purring started, and he grabbed my hand. "I think there is more in my bedroom I want to show you."

We got to his room, and as soon as the door closed, I grabbed his head and crashed my lips against his. His mouth was so different from mine, but we fit together so perfectly. His arms surrounded me, and he lifted me up, carrying me to his bed. He let me down gently, never letting his lips leave mine.

I pulled him down with me, needing his massive body on top of mine. His weight pushing me down on the soft mattress comforted me, and his purring excited me. I wanted more; I wanted all of him and I felt like I might break if he didn't give me what I craved.

"I want you to fuck me," I moaned as his mouth traveled across my cheek to nibble on my ear.

"Goddess yes. I want to fill your pussy with my cock and feel you come around me," Ira groaned.

His crude words ignited something inside of me and I could feel my pussy clench around nothing. Somewhere in the back of my mind, the sensible voice piped up, remembering his words about mated couples and babies.

"Any chance that you have a condom or something?" I asked.

"Condom?" Ira asked, tipping his head to the side, looking like an adorably confused puppy.

"Like a contraception. Birth control. A no baby insurance," I said, waving at my pussy.

"Oh. Yes. I have something," Ira said as he got off the bed.

He rumbled through his closet and came back with a small pill. I put out my hands to take it, but he popped it in his mouth and swallowed.

"This will ensure I can't get you pregnant."

"So birth control, but for men? Nice," I said.

"Yes. In my culture, we hold the responsibility for it," Ira said with a serious voice.

"So you can come inside of me?" I asked, opening my legs, needing to feel his thick cock inside of me, filling me with his cum.

"Yes," he growled, before kissing me again.

My hands went to his hair, grabbing it tight as his tongue delved into my mouth. I moaned into the kiss, so ready for him to fuck me, but Ira took it slow, kissing me as if we had all the time in the world. His tongue felt so different from a human's, and I loved it. It was rough against mine, licking me to coax mine out to play with him.

I pulled at his suit, needing to get him naked and on top of me. He growled as he unfastened it, pulling away the material so I could touch his naked skin. His hands roved over my body, pulling away the fabric until we were both naked and panting, our lips never straying too far away.

I let my hand slide down over his chest to his hardening cock. I already knew how big he was, and although I was kind of scared he might not fit, I was eager to try. Ira groaned when my hand closed around his erection, purring so loudly it vibrated in my hand. Even if it wouldn't fit, I already had other ideas on how to use it for my pleasure.

"Fuck me, please Ira," I moaned as we both came up for air.

"We need to take it slow," he growled as he slid down my body, laving his tongue over my breasts.

I moaned, grabbing his head to guide me to my puckered nipples. His rough tongue felt delicious on the delicate skin, and pleasure sparked deep inside of me.

"I don't want slow. I want you," I said, opening my legs so he could fit in between them.

"I might burst too soon," Ira panted as he kissed lower. "I need to make this good for you."

I was touched he was thinking about my pleasure too, and not just about getting his cock wet.

"This is already so good for me, Ira. It will only feel better with you inside of me."

"I need to taste you first. Make sure you are nice and wet, my Ma-, Haydée," Ira said as his mouth hovered over my pussy.

I moaned as I saw the desire burn in his eyes, and his mouth descend to my aching pussy. I wanted to bring up his slip of the tongue, but his tongue was doing things to my pussy that made my brain go to mush. His tongue flitted out, pink and long, and he pushed in between my pussy lips, giving me the most erotic lick I've ever seen.

"Delicious," Ira growled before diving in for real.

His hands grabbed my thighs to keep my legs spread wide, and he licked me like a man possessed. Moans tumbled from my lips as pleasure sparked with each flick of his tongue. The texture felt heavenly on my pussy, and I already knew he had ruined me for every other man out there. Nothing could ever compare, and nothing would ever feel as good as Ira's tongue on my pussy.

"Yes, more," I moaned, greedy with the pleasure he was giving me.

Ira licked me again, and again until it felt like it was too much. Just when I was about to ask him to stop, he focused on my clit, gently sucking on it, and making me explode with a pleasured cry. Pleasure washed over me as he murmured, happily sucking on my clit. My whole body trembled as my empty pussy clenched around nothing, aching for his cock to fill me. He let me come down from my high with the gentle laps of his tongue on my abused flesh.

"Ira, that was..."

"Exquisite," Ira growled against my pussy.

"Now fuck me," I groaned as I pulled at his shoulders.

I couldn't move his massive body if I wanted to, but he let me pull him up over my body. His mouth met mine in a passion-filled kiss, mingling his taste with mine.

"I could stay down there all day if you let me, Haydée," he murmured against my lips.

I laughed, caressing his cheeks with a brilliant smile. "I'll take you up on that offer another time. Now I need your thick cock filling my pussy."

"Goddess, I need that too," Ira growled as he positioned his cock at my entrance.

"Yes, Ira, yes," I moaned as he slowly pushed inside.

It was a tight fit, and I could feel my pussy stretch to accommodate his impressive girth. He was so big that I wasn't sure it would even fit, but as he pulled out and pushed back in, he got a bit deeper. With slow and sure thrusts, he gave me inch after delicious inch of his cock. He was wider at the base, and I could feel myself stretch more and more as he pushed in deeper until he gave me all of him.

"So good, so tight," Ira groaned as he bottomed out inside of me, and I could feel his body tremble on top of mine.

"Yes, so good," I moaned in reply. "Now fuck me."

His purring started, and I gasped as I could feel his massive cock vibrate inside of me. It was like the world's best vibrator, and when he pulled out, I could feel him drag the tip against my G-spot, almost making me combust. Pleasure sparked as sounds of desire tumbled from my lips, and when he pushed back inside, I cried out his name.

Ira groaned my name in reply as he fucked me, sparking pleasure with each thrust. His purring made everything feel more vibrant and each thrust more pleasurable. It wouldn't be long before I would tip over the edge and I wanted him to join me.

"I'm going to come," I moaned. "I need you to fill me up. Give me your cum and fill my pussy with it."

"Goddess, Haydée," Ira groaned as his tail swished behind him and his purring grew stronger.

His cock vibrated inside of me, and after a few more thrusts, my climax took over. Waves of pleasure washed over me as I called out his name. My whole body trembled and my pussy squeezed around his cock, making his groans louder.

"Come for me, Ira," I moaned as pleasure flowed through me.

Ira growled and his movements became more erratic. His cock throbbed deep inside of me, and I could feel his cum fill me, only elongating my orgasm. When the last tremors left his body, he pulled out and rolled next to me.

"Vibrating cock," I gasped as my body still trembled with aftershocks.

"Is that a good thing?" Ira asked, searching my face for any signs of displeasure.

I pulled his head to me for a kiss and moaned against his lips. "If it was any better, I might have died of a pleasure overload."

His toothy grin was back, and he pulled me into his embrace. We lay in his bed, cuddling, when a beeping sound pulled Ira away from me. His tail stayed curled around me as he sat up.

"Zion is calling a crew meeting. Let's go," he said, and I groaned in reply.

I wanted to lie in his bed for a week, but we needed to hear what Zion had to say. We got dressed and arrived at the dining hall where everyone was already sitting. Maia smiled and waved at me, and I waved back hesitantly. Zion stood in the middle, nodding at us when we took a seat.

"Good, everyone is here. I talked to the commission, and they agreed that Haydée did not need to testify. Taking into account multiple requests, I have decided we will go to Earth. I am giving everyone a week of leave to go visit family and take a break."

"Yes!" Maia said. "I can't wait for my friends to meet our kids and Levix."

Zion nodded. "I will leave the navigating to Altair and Vivian."

"If we adjust course, I estimate we will arrive on Earth in three days," Altair said in a calm voice.

Relief filled me. I was so happy to be going home and finally be able to talk to my maman, and I couldn't wait to show Ira around.

Chapter 7

We arrived at my apartment a few days later. The trip had gone smoothly and the transfer to the Earth's atmosphere with my body getting used to the gravity again had gone great.

"Welcome to my space," I said holding my arms up and twirling around.

It might be small, but it was all mine. "Don't look at the mess. I wasn't expecting company when I got abducted," I joked, happy I could laugh about it now.

"It is very you," Ira said with the toothy grin I had grown to love.

I looked around trying to see it through his eyes. My apartment was completely decorated with dark gray tones and floral accents. It might be too girly for his taste, but I liked it.

"Is that a good thing?" I asked.

"The best," Ira said as he pulled me into his arms and twirled around in my apartment with me.

I giggled loving how free he was with his touches and laughs. I was falling head over heels for this alien and everything he did made me care for him even more.

"Oh, I almost forgot why I needed to come back," I said with a laugh after he set me down.

I walked to my nightstand where my phone and glasses lay exactly as I left them there a few days ago. I knew it hadn't been long, but it felt like a lifetime ago and a different Haydée had gone to bed that night.

I pulled off the contraption Levix had made and put my round glasses on, sighing in relief. It might not give me a 360 view, but I much preferred it, finally feeling like myself again. I turned towards Ira to see what he thought of them.

"So, what do you think?" I asked.

"Of what?" Ira asked.

"Of my glasses," I said, gesturing at my face, now adorned by the round spectacles.

"Oh. What should I think? They are part of you, and I enjoy every part of you, my Ma- Haydée," Ira said, swallowing the M-word he was about to say.

"Good," I said with a nod, picking up my phone next.

I wanted to address the M- word, but I knew my mother would be worried. I only had a few texts and one missed call from my maman, so I immediately called her, explaining everything that happened. She was relieved to hear from me, and when I said I met a gorgeous alien, she was happy for me. We made plans to meet up later and for her to meet Ira. We closed off with air kisses and I love you.

I turned towards Ira, who looked at me with a strange expression on his face.

"What is it?" I asked, stepping towards him.

His tail immediately pulled me close to him, and his arms surrounded me.

"It sounded like you both care for each other deeply."

"Of course," I said with a laugh. "She is my maman and all the family I have left."

"My only family is the crew," Ira said with a sad smile.

"What happened to your birth family?" I asked.

"They all died in the war when I was young. I served my time until it ended and left it all behind to work odd jobs here and there on a spaceport. It was an okay life until Zion found me and took me in, giving me a family again after being on my own for so long."

"I'm sorry that happened to you," I said.

I couldn't imagine living through something like that and I could see it was hard for him to talk about.

Ira shrugged. "Everything happens for a reason, and it led me to you."

"I'm happy you found me," I said.

"I am too," Ira said.

The sun was setting, and I stepped towards my massive window to overlook the city I'd grown up in. Ira came up behind me, hugging me close to his body, his tail curling around one of my legs. Little lights dotted the city as far as the eye could see, making it sparkle like a diamond.

"It is a beautiful world that you live in," Ira said.

"It is. This is the first apartment I lived in on my own, and it was scary at first, but I have grown to love it so much."

"I can see why."

Turning around in his arms, I smiled up at him. I was ready for a new adventure with him, traveling the galaxy together. I caressed his cheek and Ira closed his eyes, purring.

"It doesn't matter where we are, as long as you are with me," I said as his purring relaxed me. "I want to talk to you about something."

"Okay," Ira said, still purring.

"What does it mean to be Mates?" I asked.

He hadn't said the word to me yet, but I needed to know what it meant before he met my mother and I would grow even more attached to him. His eyes flew open, and I could see so many emotions swimming around in them.

"Mates?" he asked.

"Yes. I overheard Zion say it to you, and you almost slipped up a few times, but you never came forward with it. I figure it was something like being husband and wife, like Maia and Levix, and I really, really like you a lot, but I need to know where we stand before you meet my maman."

I was rattling, and the words tumbled from my mouth as my tone grew more and more agitated. Ira stared at me in wonder, his mouth slowly curving in a grin. I could see his teeth gleaming in the dim light, and I loved how different he was from me.

"You really, really like me?" he asked.

I rolled my eyes. Of course, he had focused on that part of my rambling, and not on the question at hand.

"Yes, I might even be starting to fall in love with you."

"I love you, my Mate," he said in a deep rumble. "If you accept me, I will forever love you until the day I die."

"So it is as easy as accepting you, and we are Mates?" I asked.

"We will always be Mates, but if you don't want me, I can leave you alone. It won't hurt you."

"Of course I want you. I've never wanted anyone as much as I want you. I can't imagine not being with you are not hearing your purring at night."

"I want you too, Haydée, my Mate."

He picked me up and kissed me. I moaned into the kiss, loving his mouth on mine as he walked me towards the bed. Even though we only had sex a few days ago, I was already craving his cock again.

"I need you," I moaned.

"I need you too, Haydée," Ira said as he put me down on the bed. "I need to taste you, smell you, feel you."

"Yes," I moaned as he pulled my clothes off.

I had gotten some clothes from Maia, but I wanted to feel his naked body on top of mine. I craved his touch, his tongue, and his cock. He opened my legs wide with his hands, scrapping my sensitive skin with his sharp claws. In moments I was naked, and panting, so ready for his mouth on my pussy.

Ira hovered over me, grinning and looking at my achingly empty pussy. His cute nose crinkled as he inhaled my scent, and his purring started.

"Please Ira," I moaned, ready to beg for his mouth on me.

"You are so beautiful when you beg for your pleasure, my Mate," he groaned before he dove down between my thighs and licked me.

"Oh Ira," I moaned as his tongue slipped between my pussy lips, lapping at my entrance.

He slid his tongue inside my pussy, fucking me with the amazing appendage that made my toes curl. His purring made his tongue vibrate inside of me, only enhancing my pleasure. I could feel the pleasure slowly rise inside of me with every thrust of his tongue. I grabbed his head, letting my fingers glide over his triangular ears, making him shiver.

His tongue focused on my clit and my back came off the bed. Pleasure flowed through me as he sucked on my pleasure bud. A scream tore from my throat as my orgasm washed over me. My pussy clenched around nothing, and I ached to be filled by his cock.

"Fuck me," I moaned, reaching for his shoulders.

"Goddess, yes," Ira groaned as he sat up, licking his lips like a cat who just got the milk.

He pulled a small box out of his pants and popped it open. It was filled with the small round contraceptive pills he needed to take to prevent pregnancy.

I quirked an eyebrow and asked. "How long do you think we are staying in Paris and how much sex do you want us to have?"

Ira grinned, biting his bottom lip and looking all kinds of sexy. "As long as you'll have me."

"Hmm, I might not let you leave. I am growing used to having a vibrating tongue and cock at my disposal."

Ira chuckled, swallowing the pill and pulling off his clothes. My breath hitched as he freed his gorgeous cock from its confinements. I loved the color, the size, and the shape of it. I never considered a cock beautiful before, but Ira's cock was a work of art.

He got back on the bed, completely naked, and pulled me closer to him by my legs. I moaned as I felt his claws dig into my skin, leaving his mark on me. He positioned his cock at my entrance, purring so loudly it vibrated against my clit. Pleasure flowed through me as my pussy clenched, so eager for his cock. Ira didn't let me wait long and pushed inside of my entrance.

I gasped as he stretched my pussy to accommodate his girth. Slowly he sunk inside of me, giving me inch after delicious inch of his cock.

"Yes, Ira, more," I moaned, scratching at his shoulder to try to pull him in deeper.

His groans and purring mixed together in a beautiful sound filled with pleasure. He pulled back, making me mewl in disappointment, and thrust back inside, sparking pleasure deep inside of my pussy. Every thrust felt so good. Sounds left me I've never made before. My hands scrambled for his shoulders, trying to keep him close to me as his hips moved at a maddening pace.

It felt amazing, but I knew I needed just a little bit more to make me come. I couldn't get to my clit with his body so close to mine.

"Pull my legs up," I moaned, and he immediately grabbed them.

Ira pulled them high, shifting our position, and thrust back inside of me. A hot spark of pleasure pulsed through me as his cock hit a spot deep inside of me I've never been able to reach before. A strangled sound of pleasure left me as he did it again and again. My hands gripped my bedding tight as Ira fucked me harder.

"Good?" he asked, looking at me with a knowing smile.

Every thrust hit my G-spot with his vibrating cock. I couldn't even reply if I wanted to. Too much pleasure flowed through me, and my body felt like it was on fire. My pussy clenched around his amazing cock as Ira fucked the words right out of me. I made sounds of encouragement and pleasure and he seemed to understand their meaning.

As the pleasure inside of me grew, my sounds became more urgent, and Ira increased his pace. I couldn't hold back my orgasm even if I wanted to. It was too good, too much, and too perfect with him. He thrust inside of me, and held still for a moment, pushing his vibrating cock right at my G-spot, and I broke. A needy sound of pleasure left me as my pussy clenched around his cock, as if trying to keep it inside of me.

Ira growled and I could feel his cock throb as he bit his lip, his face contorted with pleasure. My orgasm washed over me and I felt so much pleasure my whole body vibrated with it. My muscles clenched and a hoarse cry of pleasure tore from my throat.

Ira's cock pulsed inside of me, filling me with his cum, only enhancing my pleasure. I loved looking at him as he lost himself in pleasure, giving me his seed, and heightening my pleasure. I wished I could freeze this moment in time with him, where we were both free of worries and just filled with pleasure.

When he gave me the last of his cum, and the tremors of my orgasm faded away, he pulled out. Ira turned in the bed and pulled me in his arms, covering me with his tail.

"I'm never letting you go, my Mate," Ira murmured in my hair, and I moaned in agreement.

Chapter 8

Our week together flew by and before I knew it, it was the last day of our time together in Paris. I wanted to remember our time forever, and the best way to do that was to end with a good memory so we ordered sushi and spent the day in bed together. I had truly grown to love Ira in the short time we've known each other.

We were lying on my bed together, with my head on his stomach. My hand traveled over his tail, petting the soft fur as Ira played with my curls.

"It is cute that you have so little hair," he murmured, winding a single curl around his finger.

"I don't have little hair," I said. "You just have a lot."

"I am quite proud of the amount of hair I have. Even just a bit less, and I would have been the laughingstock of my people."

"Good thing I like it," I said. "I quite like all of you, hair and all."

"All of me?" Ira asked, his voice a touch hoarser and I could feel him purr against me.

He was so cute. All of his emotions were written on his face, and his purring always signaled to me whenever he was in the mood. I turned my head towards him, giving him my best seductive smile before moving over to his cock.

I petted him through the fabric of his pants, feeling him harden underneath my touch as his purring increased. I couldn't get enough of him. Even after a mostly sex-filled week, I still craved his cock as much as I did on the first day. I wondered if that feeling would ever fade, but seeing as every single time with him was better than the last, I didn't think so.

Pulling the fabric down, I freed his cock, almost moaning when its full glory was revealed. My mouth was already watering for his taste, and I didn't deprive myself of it. I grabbed it and pulled the tip to my lips. Ira groaned as I let my tongue glide around his cock head, loving his taste filling my mouth.

"Goddess, Haydée, I adore your tongue," he groaned.

I pulled his cock in further, caressing the rest of it with my hand. I loved giving him pleasure and hearing the sounds he made. Arousal coursed through me as more of his taste filled my mouth. His tail pushed between my legs, and I moaned as it moved over my pussy.

"Use my tail for your own pleasure," Ira said.

I sucked harder on his cock as I pulled his tail closer to me, applying the right pressure over my clit. I loved the fur tickling my thighs, and the warm, solid feeling of his tail in between my legs. Ira's purring grew louder, and the vibrations traveled through me, only increasing my pleasure. It was like having the world's biggest vibrator between your legs, trying to get you off.

"You're so beautiful with my cock in your mouth and my tail between your legs," Ira growled.

I moaned in response, increasing my movements, and sucking harder, wanting him to explode in my mouth.

"So good, too good," Ira groaned as his whole body trembled and I could feel his cock throb in my mouth.

I moaned around his cock, and moments later, he exploded with a pleasured groan. His seed filled my mouth, and I swallowed it down greedily as I gently caressed his throbbing cock. It was too much to swallow all of it, so some of it spilled out of my mouth. I loved giving him pleasure, and I loved having his taste in my mouth, and his scent on my skin. With gentle caresses, I coaxed the last of his seed out of his cock, until he let out a satisfied groan.

Ira pulled me up his body, kissing every part he encountered until I was almost at his shoulders. I giggled, holding myself steady on the headboard of the bed.

"Sit on my face, my Mate," Ira growled. "I need to taste you."

No sane woman would ever say no to that, so I moaned in response. His delicious mouth immediately made contact with my pussy, sparking pleasure deep inside of me. I loved the texture of his tongue and the things he could do with it. He lapped up my juices, moaning as my taste filled his mouth, sticking his tongue deep inside of me to get as much of them out. I moaned, my pussy clenching around his tongue as pleasure filled me.

Ira ate me out as if I was his last meal, and he never wanted it to end. His hands were on my thighs to keep them spread wide and his tail was at my back, offering me support to sit up. Every swipe of his tongue sparked pleasure and made me moan.

Ira purred against my pussy, making vibrations flow through me, only enhancing my pleasure. It was too good, and I knew I wouldn't last long. As if he felt the same, he focused on my clit, flicking his tongue over it, and circling around it until I was a moaning mess. Just when I was about to beg him for my orgasm, he positioned his mouth over my pleasure bud and sucked.

I came, screaming his name as pleasure washed over me. My pussy clenched as my whole body trembled and waves of pleasure filled my senses. More of my juices came out of me, and Ira lapped them up, murmuring happily.

With a gasp, I let myself fall on his body. "Amazing," I moaned.

"Delicious," Ira replied.

Before I could say anything in reply, my alarm beeped, signaling the end of our time together in Paris.

"It's time to pack," I said, stretching out as his tail surrounded my waist.

I petted it with a laugh. "You can't keep me in bed forever, Ira."

He pulled me back, surrounding me with his limbs and tail, purring against me. "I can try."

Ira tried his best, but after a few tickles and laughs, he released me so I could pack up the rest of my stuff. Most of it was already on the way to my maman. All that was left was what I wanted to take back to the ship. I had limited myself to two bags, one filled with my curl products and clothes, and the other for sentimental value.

Ira's gaze followed me around my small space as I picked up the last of my stuff. I would miss my apartment, but I was ready for this next chapter of my life together with Ira, my Mate.

As I looked around my space for the last time, silently saying goodbye, Ira pulled me into his warm, soft embrace. His comforting scent surrounded me, making me feel grounded. He buried his head in my curls, inhaling as if he wanted to memorize my scent.

"I don't want to leave," Ira mumbled in my ear.

I laughed, patting his arm. "I'll admit we had some good times here, but we can always come visit. There is still so much from Paris I want to show you."

His arms tightened around me and I could feel his heart beat a thousand miles a minute. I hugged him back, caressing him in soothing movements, loving the feel of his soft fur underneath my hands.

"I don't want to leave you," Ira said.

I pulled back, my eyebrows furrowed. "What do you mean? We are going to your ship, right? You're not going to leave me after the week we had, after the things I shared with you?" I asked, my heart speeding up. "You even met my maman." And he had received the stamp of approval.

His expression mimicked mine as confusion hung heavily between us. "You are coming with me to my ship? I thought you wanted to stay on Earth?"

"I never said I wanted to stay. I said I wanted to go back. I needed to get my glasses and say my goodbyes to my maman and friends."

A soft purring came from his chest as his face lit up with a toothy grin. "You want to be with me?"

"Of course, you silly cat. What did you think I was going to do? Leave you after the best week of my life? We are mates, right?" I asked the last question hanging heavily in the air.

"Yes, of course, but I could never ask you to leave your family behind. I was going to stay with you here, but I didn't know how to tell the crew yet."

I shook my head, laughing. "Why did you think I was packing up and sending stuff to my maman for safekeeping? Why do I have my bags packed to join you on the ship?"

He sputtered, holding out his hands in surrender. "I thought it was a strange Earth custom I didn't know about!"

Another laugh bubbled up inside of me. Maybe we should have talked more than just having amazing sex all the time, even though I didn't regret a second of it.

"You silly cat," I said. "I quit my job. I leased out my apartment and packed all of my things. I am going with you, whether you like it or not."

Ira's mouth curved into that delicious, toothy grin I had grown to love so much. He pulled me towards him, encircling my waist with his tail.

"My Mate," Ira murmured, caressing my cheek. "My beautiful, brave Mate."

I smiled until my cheek hurt. I've never had anyone look at me the way Ira did. I knew that wherever we were or whatever we encountered, he would protect me.

A ping from his communication device broke our shared silence. As he checked the message, his smile grew wider.

"Zion needs more time to persuade his Bond Mate to stay with him, so he is giving us all an extra week of leave."

"That is great!" I said. "That way I can show around Paris some more and we can have all the loud and wild sex we want."

"My perfect Mate," Ira murmured before kissing me.

"I love you, Ira," I said, needing to hear him say it.

"I love you too, Haydée," Ira said with the biggest grin I had ever seen, showing all of his dangerous fangs that I had grown to love.

THE END

Epilogue

One year later

"NEVER AGAIN," IRA GRUNTED as he lifted me up as soon as I entered the ship.

"What? We caught the bad guy," I said with a laugh.

"Too dangerous. Something could have happened to you," he growled as he ran to our room.

I waved to the rest of the crew as we passed, giggling the entire way. It was cute how protective he was over me. I knew he was only a short way away while I was bait in our latest mission for the interplanetary police. Everything had gone exactly as planned, and we finally rounded up the last of the smuggling rings that abducted humans from Earth.

I knew there would probably be new ones coming to fill the void, but it felt good to have been part of something like this. It helped me get over my fear of being abducted and made me feel safer in the vast expanse of space we traveled together as a crew.

Ira dropped me on the bed, tearing off my suit. "Need you, my Mate," he growled as his purring started.

"Yes, fuck me, now," I moaned, opening my legs wide for him.

"Need to taste you first," Ira said before diving down in between my legs.

I moaned his name as his tongue made contact with my aching pussy. My pussy was already wet, and his tongue sparked pleasure deep inside of me. He licked me with the flat of his tongue, teasing my clit until I cried out with pleasure. My Mate knew my every pleasure point, and he licked me until I was a moaning mess, but I needed to come with his cock inside of my aching pussy.

"Fuck me, Ira," I moaned, desperate for his cock inside of me.

Ira growled, licking me and ignoring my request. He pulled my legs wider, pushing his tongue inside of me, fucking me with it until I came with a pleasured cry. He pulled it out, focusing on my clit with his deliciously textured tongue, only making my pleasure bigger. My orgasm washed over me as his tongue did things to me only he could do. My body trembled as my pussy squeezed around nothing, achingly empty and ready for his cock.

"I need your cock. Now," I moaned.

After he licked me from an inch of my life, he sat up, grabbing one of the birth control pills from our nightstand. I grabbed his hand before he could put it in his mouth and smiled.

"What if we did it without?" I asked.

"You want to try breeding?" Ira asked, his voice dropping an octave.

"If you are okay with it? Knowing there are no aliens out there abducting humans made me feel safe again, and maybe it is time to expand our little family?"

"It would make me the happiest Felicion in the galaxy," Ira said with his toothy grin.

"Good, now fuck me and fill me with your seed. Your Mate needs to be bred," I said.

Ira groaned, positioning himself in between my legs. He pushed his cock at my entrance and thrust inside of me, filling me with one move. Even with the wetness of my orgasm, it was still a tight fit. Every time with Ira felt so amazing, I had to hold myself back from coming too soon. His purring vibrated through his body and mine, pleasuring my pussy from the inside out.

"Goddess, Haydée. You feel so good I might burst too soon," Ira groaned in my hair.

"Yes, fill me with your seed. Breed me."

Ira growled, pulling back and thrusting inside of me, making pleasure spark. It wouldn't be long before I came again, and I wanted him to come with me. I loved his vibrating cock deep inside of me and needed him to fill me with his seed.

"More, harder, fuck me, Ira, please. Breed me, my Mate," I moaned with my hands in his hair, scratching behind his ears.

His whole body trembled as he fucked me harder, giving me everything I needed and more. Pleasure pulsed through my body with each thrust. I loved him with every fiber of my being and every day with him was like a gift that I treasured with everything I had.

"Haydée, come for me, my Mate," Ira growled as I could feel his cock throb deep inside of me.

He held still, vibrating against my G-spot, making sparks fly deep inside of me. Pleasure washed over me as I came, screaming his name. Ira followed me close behind, filling me with his seed, only prolonging my climax.

"My gorgeous, beautiful Mate," he murmured, purring against me.

"I love you so much, Ira."

"I love you too, Haydée," Ira said, pulling out of me, and pulling me into his embrace, surrounding me with his arms and tail.

Who knew that getting abducted by alien blobs would result in me finding the love of my life, my Alien Mate?

THE END

Authors Note

I absolutely love Ira! I mean, just look at the front cover art! I had the art far before I even started writing his story and I just kept looking at the art trying to convey who he was and how he would meet his Mate.

I knew I wanted to do something with miscommunication and some different language representation. I am from Belgium myself which is a trilingual country, so I knew I wanted to put a French FMC in it. Giving Haydée glasses was inspired by a FB comment from someone who asked for recs for an FMC with glasses and I realized I hadn't written one! I used to wear glasses so I really needed to have it represented in one of my own books.

Let's talk about his ahum, equipment, wink wink. Purring, vibrating, and a big dong? What more can a girl want? I loved writing it and making up all of the fun stuff.

I want to give a special thanks to Courtney and Ada who betaread this story and made it even better! Thank you so much!

I also had some amazing NSFW art created by misteluna who also created the cover art! This artprint and a naughty sticker with Ira full frontal are available in my Etsy Shop!

Etsy Shop: https://www.etsy.com/be/shop/SteamyPublishing

Anyway, I hope you enjoyed the story! Please leave a rating and / or a review if you did!

About the author

Lilith Leana writes what she loves; Monster, fantasy, and sci-fi erotica.

Born and raised in Belgium, she devours ebooks as if it heals her. In her day job she loves to organize, plan and make schedules for other people, but when the night falls she can let loose with her fantasies which star all kinds of Non-Human and Human couplings.

YOU CAN ALSO FIND ME on:

New Author Website: https://lilithleana.wordpress.com/

New Newsletter! Sign Up to be kept up to date about my new releases, sales, character art, and giveaways: Sign Up Form[1]

Instagram: https://www.instagram.com/lilithleana/

Etsy Shop: https://www.etsy.com/be/shop/SteamyPublishing

Or you can email me: lilith.leana666@gmail.com

DEAR READER

If you enjoyed this book, please consider leaving a review. Indie writers depend on reviews to keep writing and publishing.

Thank you so much ❤

Lilith

---

1.   https://dashboard.mailerlite.com/forms/533589/95138330138642151/share

Also by the author

Alien Erotica

<u>Bonded to the Purple Alien</u>[1]
<u>The Stowaway Mate</u>[2]
<u>My Alien Pen Pal</u>[3]

Monster Novellas

<u>My Ghostly Lover</u>[4]
<u>My Orc Mate</u>[5]

---

1. https://books2read.com/u/bMzOl7

2. https://books2read.com/u/mZpzPe

3. https://books2read.com/u/mdwKwW

4. https://books2read.com/u/3J6dxJ

5. https://books2read.com/u/3yd90L

Brief summaries of other Alien Erotica titles by Lilith Leana

The Stowaway Mate[1]

Desperate to escape her slave master, Maia stows away on a cargo ship, only to be discovered by the disgruntled alien crew. When one alien goes into heat, claiming her as his mate, she faces the choice to stay or go back to her life as a slave. If she stays, she'll need to help the devil-like alien through his heat. Maia keeps an eye out for any opportunity to reclaim her freedom but slowly develops feelings for the first alien to treat her like an equal.

The moment Levix catches the alluring fragrance of the petite human woman, he realizes with certainty that she is his Mate. His heat takes over his body and mind and only she can help him.

When Levix's heat is over and the opportunity arrives, will Maia choose freedom or her Mate?

My Alien Pen Pal[2]

Against all odds, a lonely scientist and a soft-spoken Alien find each other in the vast expanse of space.

After seven years of isolation in her research center, Vivian's Pen Pal, Altair, surprises her with a planet-side visit. She is amazed to meet the golden-skinned alien she has been talking to for so long. The moment Vivian feels his scorching hot touch, she doesn't care about their differences and cannot wait to discover his body.

Altair fell in love with Vivian's mind and voice, so when the opportunity presents itself, he can't wait to meet her. When they do, sparks fly, his body responds, and he does not want to leave the planet without her.

---

1. https://books2read.com/u/mZpzPe

2.   https://books2read.com/u/mdwKwW

When their time together comes to an end, will Vivian choose to continue her ten-year research or go with her Alien Pen Pal to discover galaxies together?

Bonded to the Purple Alien[3]

Jenny wakes up on a strange planet, not remembering anything. The only other occupant seems to be a handsome four-armed, purple alien who needs to take in her essence to be able to communicate with her. As she grows closer to the alien and starts to remember more their bond grows stronger.

Astor sees the cute alien and instantly knows she is his. He will bond with her by his customs, and never let go. When it appears that human bonding ceremonies entail a bit more than he is used to, he is all in.

---

3.   https://books2read.com/u/bMzOl7